T0014613

Trainer's Mini Exploration Guide to Hoenn

Trainer's Mini Exploration Guide to Hoenn

INSIGHT
EDITIONS

SAN RAFAEL • LOS ANGELES • LONDON

CONTENTS

Welcome to Hoenn!

Hoenn is home to 135 newly discovered Pokémon, as well as plenty of familiar faces—that's a lot of Pokémon to see and catch! From the wide-open skies above to the depths of the expansive ocean, there are all sorts of wondrous and mysterious Pokémon just waiting to be found, and this guide will get you started on your **journey to catch them all**!

TREECKO #252

If a larger foe were to stare down Treecko, this Pokémon wouldn't give an inch, instead **glaring** right back at its opponent while remaining **cool, calm, and collected**. If the situation does come to a fight, however, Treecko is able to scale vertical walls using small hooks on the bottom of its feet, then let loose an attack by slamming its thick tail into its opponent!

Ash's Treecko once lived in a grand tree in the middle of a forest, but when Ash found it, the tree was **dying**.

While the other Treecko living there had given up and planned to leave the tree, Ash's Treecko remained, caring for the tree **In hopes it could be restored**.

"**Now it's my turn to protect this tree! Whatever happens, I'll stay with it until the end!**"
—Treecko, translated by Meowth

GROVYLE #253

Well adapted to life in the trees, Grovyle is a **master climber**, and no Pokémon can hope to keep up with a Grovyle in the forest, no matter how fast they are. When Grovyle wants to instead remain still and unseen, it uses the leaves on its body to camouflage itself among the canopy.

Just after evolving, Ash's Grovyle showed off its **brand-new attack**, Leaf Blade, by using the leaves on its arms to cut a new twig from a tree to keep in its mouth.

But these sharp leaves can also be utilized in battle for some **fierce attacks**!

SCEPTILE #254

The seeds on Sceptile's back are full of nutrients that feed and revitalize trees. It lives in forests and raises the trees in its home with loving care. That doesn't make it a pushover, however! In combat, Sceptile can **quickly dart** between trees to leap down on its foe from above or behind before **striking** with the sharp leaves on its body.

TORCHIC #255

With soft, fluffy down and an ever-warm inner flame, Torchic is perfect for cuddling up with. But watch out—the flame sac in its belly that produces this warmth can also be used by Torchic to exhale flames that exceed 1,800 degrees Fahrenheit! It can even **launch fireballs** that leave the opponent smoking and charred!

COMBUSKEN #256

By running through fields and mountains, Combusken builds up the muscles in its legs. Through this intense training, it develops a mastery and strength that enables it to unleash **powerful kicks**—as many as ten kicks in just one second!

When Ash's Corphish took a beating from some angry Breloom to protect May's Torchic, Torchic **evolved** into Combusken and went toe to toe with the Breloom leader to return the favor!

BLAZIKEN #257

All of its training as a Combusken has paid off—now that it's evolved, Blaziken uses its powerful legs to make huge leaps capable of clearing even a thirty-story building! When fighting, it ignites the flames on its wrists, its punches then leaving its foes **scorched** and **blackened**.

MUDKIP #258

The fin atop Mudkip's head is **incredibly sensitive**, able to sense the movements of the surrounding water and air. Its fin is so keen, in fact, that Mudkip can detect what's going on around it, even when completely unable to see!

Ash and his friends stumbled upon the land of Old Man Swamp, who had created an artificial marshland for raising Mudkip.

Baby Mudkip are very **cute** and **small**—but that meant that when Team Rocket broke the dam Old Man Swamp had made, they couldn't swim against the current!

MARSHTOMP #259

Marshtomp has the **strange trait** of being able to **swim faster in mud** than in water—perhaps that's why it can often be found playing in the mud on beaches when the tide is low! When it wants to, however, Marshtomp is more than capable of making trips onto land. Its body is covered in a thick film that enables it to leave the water, and its legs have developed so that it's able to walk around on just its hind legs!

SWAMPERT #260

Evolution has only made Swampert's senses keener—
it can now detect oncoming storms by sensing the
slight differences in waves and the wind with its fins.
To protect itself and its beachside nest, it then uses its
mighty strength to make itself a shelter out of
boulders that can weigh more than a ton!

ARON #304

The steel armor that covers Aron's body is **shed** when it evolves, and ancient people would collect the shed armor and put it to use in their day-to-day lives. But in order to produce that armor to start with, Aron has to eat plenty of iron ore—sometimes it even nibbles on railroad tracks!

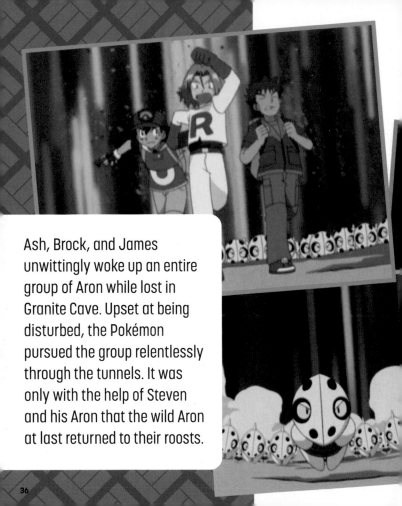

Ash, Brock, and James unwittingly woke up an entire group of Aron while lost in Granite Cave. Upset at being disturbed, the Pokémon pursued the group relentlessly through the tunnels. It was only with the help of Steven and his Aron that the wild Aron at last returned to their roosts.

Steven also had Aron at his side to help him find **rare stones**, and it was Aron who finally sniffed out the Fire Stone Steven had been searching for!

LAIRON #305

Lairon is **fiercely territorial**, and close inspection of the Pokémon reveals scratches and dents all over its steel armor from slamming into foes during disputes. In the past, Lairon often came into conflict with humans, as they made their homes in mountains with fresh spring water and plenty of iron ore.

AGGRON #306

Aggron's horn is **sharp** enough to pierce thick sheets of metal, and it fights by slamming into foes horn-first to make them faint. There was even once a king who wore a helmet in the shape of Aggron's head to try and channel this Pokémon's strength!

The Hoenn region is home to a great deal of water—and plenty of Water-type Pokémon! In fact, **twenty-eight new Water-type** Pokémon have been discovered in the Hoenn region. Many can be found easily by just surfing the waves and exploring the vast seas!

WAILMER #320

WAILORD #321

SHARPEDO #319

CARVANHA #318

KECLEON #352

Kecleon's **color changes** for a number of reasons—not only as an indicator of mood or health, but also to hide among its surroundings! However, if Kecleon goes unnoticed for too long, it gets sad and chooses to never come out of hiding.

"Wow, the same type
of Pokémon in two
designer colors!"
—Misty

Ash met a couple of Kecleon that could hide almost perfectly within their environment—except for the **red zigzag pattern** around their midsections, which can't change color at all!

ZIGZAGOON #263

Zigzagoon is covered in bristly fur that it rubs against trees to mark its territory. **Very curious**, it often runs back and forth in a zigzag fashion between things that catch its interest. With all this aptitude for investigation, Zigzagoon is likely to be able to find most anything you've lost!

LINOONE #264

When chasing prey, Linoone makes use of **sharp** claws and **explosive** speed. It's capable of reaching up to sixty miles per hour when moving in a straight line, but can't make turns while running, so winding paths are a bit of a struggle!

When Kimmy's friend Tokin evolved from Zigzagoon into Linoone, it started running off and taking things to create a **stash of round or rare items**.

Unfortunately, it also stole from people that were passing through the area—including May's Poké Balls for Bulbasaur and Beautifly, which it **held in its cheeks** rather than stashing away!

CASTFORM #351

Castform's appearance **changes with the weather**, with rougher weather leaving Castform with a rougher attitude. It's not Castform's fault, though—the shift comes as a result of a chemical reaction to temperature and humidity, not because Castform chooses to change!

Castform has **four forms** it changes between: a normal form for cloudy weather, one for rain, one for hail and snow, and one for sunny skies. Castform can change in a moment—one Castform that Ash met cycled through all four forms over the course of a single day!

TRAPINCH #328

Trapinch makes its nests in the desert, forming sloped, conical pits to catch its prey. Once something falls in, there's **no escape** from the jaws of a hungry Trapinch waiting at the bottom!

VIBRAVA #329

By rubbing its wings together, Vibrava produces sound waves that **can't be heard**, but can certainly be felt—if you've got a sudden, severe headache for no reason, chances are there's a Vibrava about!

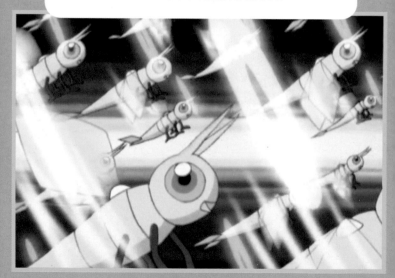

When the Trapinch that live in the Trapinch Underground Labyrinth are **ready to evolve**, they gather at a huge underground lake.

There, they participate in a **mass Evolution** event before the whole swarm of new Vibrava take off into the skies to live their new lives aboveground!

FLYGON #330

Flygon **hides in sandstorms** of its own making, rarely venturing into places where it can be found.

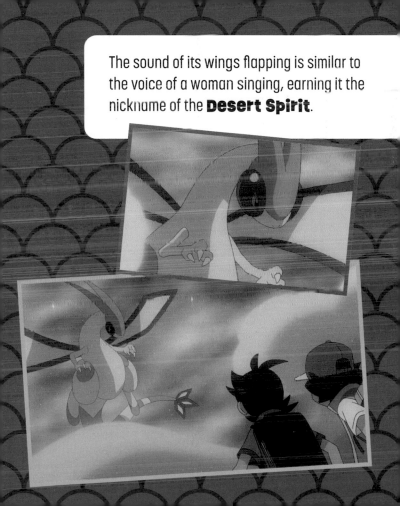

The sound of its wings flapping is similar to the voice of a woman singing, earning it the nickname of the **Desert Spirit**.

"I feel like it's singing to me."
—Ash

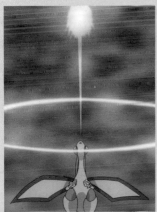

When a strange sandstorm appeared at Mauville City, drawing people in with a **mysterious song**, Ash and Coh were sent to investigate. Turned out, a Flygon had made the sandstorm, possibly hoping to make a habitat for itself in the miniature desert it had created!

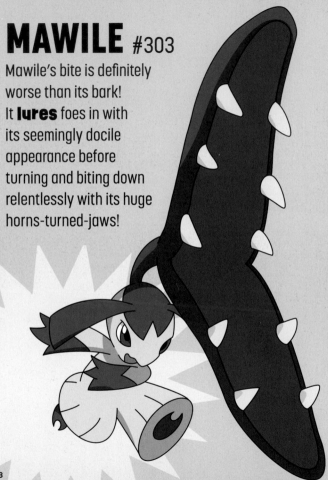

MAWILE #303

Mawile's bite is definitely worse than its bark! It **lures** foes in with its seemingly docile appearance before turning and biting down relentlessly with its huge horns-turned-jaws!

69

Samantha's Mawile **wasn't afraid** to take a Bite out of the spiny Cacnea or even its crush Lombre, and it had some great strength—it was able to launch Corphish using just its large jaws!

FEEBAS #349

Feebas is often overlooked, as it isn't the prettiest Pokémon to look at. However, researchers have taken to studying it on account of its **incredible vitality**—this Water-type Pokémon's hardy nature allows it to survive even in very little water!

Despite what many think, there are lots of people out there who love Feebas just as it is. Parker's friend Jinny thought her Feebas, Feeby, was the cutest Pokémon ever, even before it evolved into Milotic!

"It's a shame people don't get how great Feebas is."
—Ash

Because they believed in Feeby, Ash, Goh, and Chloe
helped Jinny and Feeby train to enter a contest for
Water-type Pokémon to show everyone just how
great Feeby was!

MILOTIC #350

Unlike its previous Evolution, Milotic's beauty is moving. It has served as the subject of many art pieces, and even just a glimpse of this Pokémon is said to bring a calm to any hostility you might be feeling. Many claim that Milotic is the **most beautiful** Pokémon of them all!

Plusle and Minun are **fantastic cheerleaders**. They get very invested in their team's battles and spark all over with electricity to cheer them on. When things go poorly, Plusle cries loudly and share in its partner's loss, but Minun only gets more fired up, letting off more sparks to encourage them!

PLUSLE #311

MINUN #312

After wearing out Pikachu in a **rigged battle**, Team Rocket nearly managed to nab it, but a timely Helping Hand from Thatcher's Plusle and Minun supercharged Pikachu's Thunder attack so it could bypass Team Rocket's protection from Electric-type attacks!

While many of the Water-type Pokémon newly discovered in the Hoenn region can be seen close to the surface, some are a **little harder to find.**

RELICANTH #369

Several make their homes in the depths of the ocean, or hide away in underground rivers, **going unseen** for long periods of time!

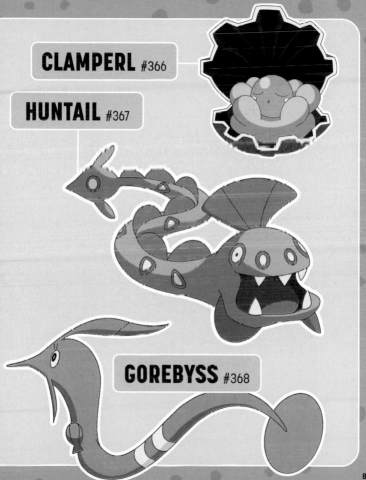

CLAMPERL #366

HUNTAIL #367

GOREBYSS #368

83

ABSOL #359

Absol's **curved horn** is acutely sensitive to the warning signs that precede natural disasters. Unfortunately, because of this many have mistaken Absol as a bringer of doom, rather than a Pokémon capable of sensing it.

When the hot springs of Lavaridge Town dried up and an Absol was sighted around the same time, the townsfolk blamed the Disaster Pokémon! But Ash and Goh discovered that Absol was actually just trying to **warn** the residents that there was more to worry about.

"I wanna believe in Absol."
—Goh

These three **mysterious titans** are believed to be ancient—but more than that, they are curiosities. With bodies made entirely of stone, ice, and a mysterious unknown metal, these Pokémon bear no organs that can be detected with even the most cutting-edge technology, but they can still move and function like normal Pokémon!

REGIROCK #377

REGICE #378

REGISTEEL #379

LATIAS #380

Latias is an **incredibly intelligent** Pokémon, able to understand human speech, and also highly sensitive to the emotions of people. Covered in glass-like down, Latias can refract light in order to change its appearance. But if it senses any hostility, it ruffles its feathers and shrieks shrilly in an attempt to intimidate its would-be opponent.

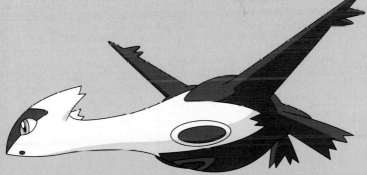

LATIOS #381

Much like Latias, its counterpart, Latios has **great intelligence** and can understand human speech. Although it can make others see images of what it has seen or created in its imagination, Latios only truly opens its heart to a Trainer with a compassionate spirit.

"Latios took out Sceptile
with just one move! To say
Latios is strong
Is an understatement!"
—announcer

93

Ash often trained his Pokémon with a **focus on speed**, but in the semifinals of the Sinnoh League he faced Tobias's Latios, who could not only match the speed of his Pokémon, but also brought considerable strength along with it. Latios outflew Ash's Swellow and even met Pikachu's Volt Tackle head-on with Giga Impact!

KYOGRE #382

Said to be the **personification of the sea**, Kyogre is well known for the many legends that tell of its clashes with Groudon and its attempt to gain the power of nature. The storms Kyogre can summon are so powerful they can cause the sea levels to rise.

During the conflict between Team Aqua and Team Magma at Monsu Island, the Red Orb bonded with Archie. Its power corrupted him, and he stopped caring about anything except Kyogre's power—**even his own people**!

Once the Red Orb was unbonded from Archie, Kyogre was **calmed** from its rage. No longer rampaging, the Legendary Pokémon was kind enough to rescue Ash and Pikachu from the water before returning to its home in the depths of the ocean.

GROUDON #383

As the **personification of the land**, Groudon clashes frequently with Kyogre throughout legend in an attempt to gain the power of nature. Groudon can cause magma to erupt from the ground and expand the landmasses of the world.

After Team Aqua set Kyogre free from Team Magma's ship, Ash's Pikachu managed to catch the Blue Orb and keep it from breaking—but ended up **absorbing** the artifact! Through the connection granted by the Blue Orb, Groudon was able to compel Pikachu to release it so that it could face Kyogre and calm it down from its rage.

Once the orbs were destroyed, Groudon returned to the heart of the nearby volcano, **away from human eyes**.

LEGENDARY

RAYQUAZA #384

Making its home flying in the ozone layer, Rayquaza is said to have lived for **hundreds of millions of years**, consuming meteoroids for food. However, there are legends of how this Pokémon laid to rest the ceaseless conflict between Kyogre and Groudon.

Rayquaza is **incredibly territorial** and has attacked things that stray into its home in the atmosphere, including Deoxys and Team Rocket's wayward rocket ship!

JIRACHI #385

It's said Jirachi will awaken from a thousand-year sleep if sung to in a voice of purity, and it can **grant any wish** that people desire. However, if Jirachi senses danger to itself, it can fight even while asleep!

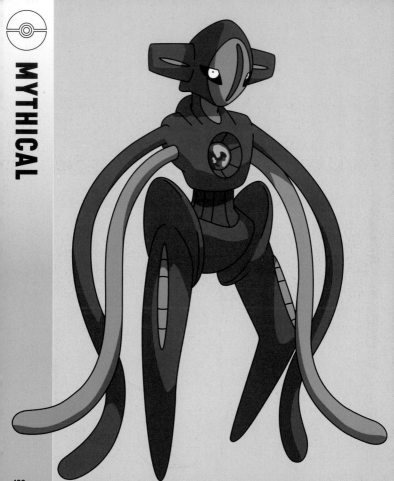

DEOXYS #386

Deoxys **originated as a virus** from space and is now a highly intelligent Pokémon that can wield powerful psychokinetic powers. It shoots lasers from the crystal in its chest—which is also believed to be this Pokémon's brain!

When a Deoxys was **struck by lightning** and crashed down on a deserted island, the native Pokémon noticed that the rocks surrounding the island resonated with the jewel left behind— because the rocks were meteorites that gave Deoxys power. With the help of Pikachu and Piplup, they collected enough pieces of the meteors to revitalize Deoxys!

> "A Pokémon that uses meteors to receive its power! That's so mysterious!"
> —Dawn

INSIGHT EDITIONS

PO Box 3088
San Rafael, CA 94912
www.insighteditions.com

f Find us on Facebook: www.facebook.com/InsightEditions
🐦 Follow us on Twitter: @insighteditions

ISBN: 978-1-64722-993-1

Text by Kay Austin

Publisher: Raoul Goff
VP, Co-Publisher: Vanessa Lopez
VP, Creative: Chrissy Kwasnik
VP, Manufacturing: Alix Nicholaeff
VP, Group Managing Editor: Vicki Jaeger
Publishing Director: Mike Degler
Designer: Leah Bloise Lauer

Associate Editor: Sadie Lowry
Editorial Assistant: Alex Figueiredo
Managing Editor: Maria Spano
Senior Production Editor: Michael Hylton
Senior Production Manager: Greg Steffen
Senior Production Manager, Subsidiary Rights:
Lina s Palma-Temena

 REPLANTED PAPER

ROOTS of PEACE

Insight Editions, in association with Roots of Peace, will plant two trees
for each tree used in the manufacturing of this book. Roots of Peace
is an internationally renowned humanitarian organization dedicated
to eradicating land mines worldwide and converting war-torn lands
into productive farms.

Manufactured in China by Insight Editions

10 9 8 7 6 5 4 3 2 1